OUR SECOND CHANCE ROMANCE

Navigating Past And Present To Find True Love

SOLOMON G. ADEGBOYE

INTRODUCTION

Within the intricate fabric of existence, only a handful of strands intertwine to create a narrative as enthralling as the opportunity to experience love once again. "Our Second Chance Romance" is a narrative of revived affection, in which the passage of time has mellowed the intense emotions of youth, enabling two individuals to reconnect in a surprising manner.

Victoria Mitchell and Joseph Carter were previously inseparable, being high school sweethearts whose love appeared fated to endure indefinitely. They exchanged aspirations, confidences, and a bond that seemed invincible. However, the unexpected nature of life caused them to separate, resulting in a collection of memories and unexpressed remorse.

After a long period of time, destiny interferes in a busy café in the city, where an unexpected meeting rekindles a passion that had never completely faded away. Victoria and Joseph are facing their rekindled emotions while also dealing with the unresolved issues from their past, the difficulties of the present, and the unknowns of the future.

This narrative encompasses more than just a tale of love; it delves into the themes of personal development, pardoning, and the bravery required to seize an opportunity for redemption. Victoria and Joseph will discover that genuine love, even if it is hidden, can be revitalised through patience, comprehension, and a touch of belief.

Accompany them as they rekindle the pleasure of being in one other's company, the anguish of facing past injuries, and the splendour of a love that was destined from the start. "Our Second Chance Romance" is a poignant and captivating journey that serves as a reminder that love, at times, warrants a second opportunity.

Chapter One

The Surprising Encounter

Serendipitous Encounter

The declining sun in the afternoon emitted a pleasant and radiant golden light that illuminated the busy streets of downtown Portland. Victoria Mitchell manoeuvred through the crowd of individuals, her mind consumed by the busy day she had experienced at the publishing company. She desired a brief period of relaxation, a location to unwind before going home. Noticing a charming café at the intersection, she concluded that a cup of coffee was precisely what she required.

Upon entering, Victoria was greeted by the scent of freshly made coffee and the gentle murmur of conversation that around her. She requested her customary beverage—an Americano with a hint of almond milk—and located a petite table adjacent to the window. She retrieved her notebook with the intention of quickly recording ideas for a new project, but her attention was immediately drawn to a rapid movement at the door.

Joseph Carter walked into the café, immediately drawing attention with his authoritative presence, even in the humble surroundings. Over the years, he underwent a transformation; his previously youthful characteristics had developed into a more mature look, and his appearance now possessed a distinct toughness. Donning a relaxed blazer and trousers, he radiated a self-assuredness that Victoria couldn't overlook. Her pulse palpitated, inundated by recollections of their intertwined history. She cast a swift glance downwards, in the hope of evading his attention.

However, destiny had alternative intentions. Joseph's eyes scanned the room and settled on Victoria. He momentarily paused, appearing to be attempting to persuade himself of her actual presence. Regaining his composure, he approached with intentional and unwavering steps.

"Victoria?" The timbre of his voice evoked a sense of familiarity and distance, a harmonious fusion of their intertwined past and the passage of time. She raised her gaze, making eye contact with him, and mustered a hesitant grin. "Joseph." It has been a considerable duration of time.

Reemergence of Past Emotions

Time seemed to pass rapidly. The café, the bustling city outside, and the people surrounding them all receded into the periphery as they confronted each other. Victoria had a surge of emotions: a longing for the past, astonishment, and a clear feeling of the love she used to have for him. She reminisced about his gaze fixed upon her, the nocturnal discussions, and the aspirations they had mutually embraced. Although the grief of their separation was intense, those recollections had remained a treasured component of her past.

Joseph also experienced the same sensation. Encountering Victoria once more evoked a surge of recollections—leisurely meals in the park, academic sessions that transformed into extensive discussions about their prospects, and the undeniable affinity they previously shared. Observing her current state, exuding grace and enhanced attractiveness, evoked a profound emotional response within him. He frequently pondered her fate, and now, she appeared before him, as though no time had elapsed.

Both individuals remained in that position, ensnared by the tumultuous waves of their feelings, until the barista interrupted their reverie by calling out Joseph's name. He seized his coffee and paused, uncertain whether to remain or depart. The lingering scars from their previous separation overshadowed the unforeseen reunion.

"May I have a moment of your time?" he inquired, his voice gentle and filled with a sense of urgency.

Victoria acknowledged by nodding and indicated the seat opposite her. "Certainly, let's meet and have a conversation to update each other."

Unwilling Dialogue

Joseph seated himself, carefully setting his coffee on the table. A tense pause ensued as they both struggled to find the appropriate words. Victoria toyed with the edge of her notebook, while Joseph indulged in a sip of his coffee, stalling for time.

"How have you been?" Victoria, at last, inquired, shattering the silence.

Joseph's smile was insincere, since it failed to reflect in his eyes. "I have been well." Engaged in professional obligations, frequently doing journeys. And what about you?"

Victoria acknowledged with a nod, while her fingers traced intricate patterns on the table. "I feel the same way." My work has been very busy, but I find it enjoyable. Engaging in productive activities is enjoyable.

They engaged in polite conversation, discussing their occupations, the locations they had travelled to, and the individuals they had encountered. The dialogue was characterised by politeness and caution, as if they were treading carefully. Both individuals were reluctant to discuss prior events, as they were concerned that it could potentially disrupt the fragile bond they were in the process of repairing.

While conversing, they inevitably observed the alterations in one another. Victoria observed a newfound maturity in Joseph, a sense of stability that had before been absent.

Joseph observed that Victoria's eyes had their original brightness, which he had always appreciated. However, he also noted a newfound depth in her stare, which seemed to represent the events she had undergone.

Their dialogue progressively became more relaxed, as the initial discomfort was replaced by a sincere interest in one other's personal experiences. They found amusement in their shared recollections, expressed wonder at the coincidences that had led them to the same café, and gradually started to unwind.

However, lurking beneath the exterior, there was a tacit inquiry: What is the next course of action? They had ceased to be the carefree adolescents who had developed romantic feelings for each other many years ago. Their life experiences had transformed them, and now they had to negotiate the intricacies of their past and present in order to comprehend the true significance of this reunion.

As the sun descended in the sky, creating elongated shadows over the café, Victoria and Joseph became aware that they had engaged in conversation for an extended period of time. They unwillingly accepted the time, both cognizant of the fact that they had to depart but hesitant to separate.

"Perhaps we could arrange another occasion to do this in the future?" Joseph proposed, his tone filled with optimism.

Victoria's face lit up with an authentic and heartfelt smile. "I would appreciate that."

They swapped contact information, a palpable feeling of excitement lingering in the atmosphere. Upon departing from the café, they each had a sense of recognition mixed with novelty—an opportunity for renewed affection that they believed had vanished permanently.

Chapter Two

Reflecting On The Past

Teenage couples that are in a romantic relationship during their time in high school

Victoria and Joseph crossed paths during their junior year of high school, a period characterised by a sense of boundless opportunities. The initial meeting occurred in the school library, when Victoria was deeply absorbed in a novel for her English class. Meanwhile, Joseph was fervently seeking a book on physics.

"Pardon me, could you please inform me of the location of the physics section?" he inquired, interrupting Victoria's focus.

She raised her gaze, feeling a little sense of annoyance due to the interruption. However, her displeasure dissipated as she observed his sincere and honest demeanour. "It is located in that direction," she stated, indicating the furthest corner of the library. "Aisle number two."

"Thank you," he responded with an appreciative grin. "My name is Joseph, just so you know."

"Victoria," she greeted, reciprocating his smile. Instantaneously, a bond was established. Their relationship flourished rapidly. Both Victoria and Joseph had a mutual passion for literature and science. They frequently spent their afternoons in the library, with Victoria engrossed in her novels and Joseph focused on his scientific endeavours. They derived comfort from one another's companionship, achieving a harmonious equilibrium between Victoria's imaginative disposition and Joseph's logical intellect.

Their encounters were uncomplicated yet enchanting. Enjoying outdoor meals in the park, taking leisurely drives at night with open car windows, and engaging in never-ending discussions beneath the starry sky. They envisioned a shared future, discussing higher education, professions, and a lifelong commitment to one another. Their love was fervent and untainted, evoking a sense of invincibility in high school sweethearts.

The End of a Relationship

Nevertheless, life has a tendency to challenge even the most resilient connections. As the final year advanced, the burdens of impending college applications and future aspirations started to exert a significant influence on them. Joseph was offered a scholarship from a renowned university located far away, whereas Victoria was determined to attend a liberal arts college that was closer to her home.

The formerly enthusiastic discussions over their future transformed into intense disputes. They attempted to reach a compromise, but the physical distance and their divergent trajectories proved to be an insurmountable barrier. The tipping point occurred on a rainy April night, shortly before the prom.

"Why are you unable to comprehend the significance of this matter to me?" Joseph expressed his dissatisfaction clearly. "This scholarship is a unique and rare opportunity that only comes once in a person's lifetime."

"And what is your stance on our situation, Joseph?" Victoria had responded, with tears cascading down her cheeks. "I am unable to abruptly relocate all of my belongings and accompany you on a journey to a different region of the country." I also possess my own aspirations." Their words reverberated through the vacant school corridor, with each word widening the divide between them. The recognition that both individuals were unwilling to compromise their aspirations for the sake of the other resulted in a profoundly distressing choice.

"I suppose this is the end," Joseph murmured softly, his eyes brimming with grief.

"Yes," Victoria murmured, her heart breaking into pieces. "I suppose it is."

They separated that evening, both burdened by the heaviness of their shattered hearts. The subsequent days were characterised by a state of emotional turmoil and remorse, as they grappled with the challenge of moving forward from the love they had believed would endure indefinitely.

Persistent Remorse

Time elapsed, although the recollections of their high school love affair remained indelibly imprinted in their memories. Victoria frequently pondered Joseph, contemplating the potential outcomes if they had taken alternative decisions. She lamented the acrimonious remarks uttered in fury, as well as the instances of obstinacy that hindered their ability to reach a compromise.

Joseph, also, was tormented by his previous experiences. He pondered the correctness of his choice to prioritise his education over their relationship. The triumph he attained in his professional life seemed empty in the absence of Victoria, with whom he could have celebrated and enjoyed it.

Upon their reunion in the present, those enduring feelings of remorse resurfaced once again. The hypothetical scenarios and potential outcomes continuously replayed in their thoughts. Both individuals pondered whether they had been insufficiently mature and inexperienced to handle the intricacies of romantic relationships and aspirations.

Victoria contemplated the aspirations they had mutually held and reflected on how effortlessly they had allowed them to fade into oblivion. She lamented her lack of perseverance in preserving their relationship, for failing to discover a solution to overcome the geographical separation. The lingering pain of their previous disagreement serves as a poignant reminder of the affection that was sacrificed in the pursuit of their respective ambitions.

Joseph, however, incessantly repeated their last talk, yearning for a means to reconcile the divide that existed between them. He lamented his lack of empathy, failing to give equal importance to Victoria's aspirations as he did to his own. The achievement he had pursued felt inadequate, eclipsed by the absence of the individual who had previously been his entire world.

Their meeting at the café had rekindled past emotional pain but also presented a faint ray of optimism. During their nostalgic conversation, Victoria and Joseph came to the realisation that the emotions they had suppressed were still quite present. The intensity of their emotional separation served as evidence of the profound nature of their affection, a love that had endured the challenges posed by both time and physical separation.

Now, presented with the prospect of a second opportunity, they were compelled to address their feelings of remorse and devise a strategy to progress. The path forward was ambiguous, but one fact was evident: their narrative was still incomplete.

Chapter Three

Reconnecting

Informal Coffee Gathering

Victoria's hands quivered slightly as she pulled the café door open, the designated meeting place for her and Joseph. As she entered, she was met with the recognisable scent of coffee, blending with the gentle hum of conversations and sporadic sound of cups being handled. She noticed Joseph seated at a table at the rear, his eyes focused on the entrance. Upon locking gazes, he displayed a smile, causing a slight alleviation of the tension in her shoulders.

"Hello," he cheerfully greeted her as she approached.

"Hello," she responded, slightly winded. "I trust that I did not cause you to wait."

"No, not in the slightest." "I have just arrived," he stated, rising to his feet to offer her a short, somewhat uncomfortable embrace before they both took their seats. They placed their drink orders—Victoria's customary Americano with a hint of almond milk and Joseph's plain black coffee—and then relaxed into a peaceful calm, each of them pausing to collect their thoughts.

Making Up for Lost Time

"How have you been?" Joseph inquired, interrupting the absence of sound. His eyes exuded authentic inquiry, evoking a surge of warmth within Victoria.

"I have been well," she responded, with a smile. "My work demands a lot of my time, but I thoroughly enjoy it." Currently, I hold the position of an editor at a publishing business.

Joseph's eyes dilated in awe. "That is truly remarkable, Victoria." Your ability to express yourself through language has always been exceptional.

Victoria's cheeks become slightly red. "Thank you." And what about yourself? Are you still frequently travelling for work?

"Yes," Joseph affirmed with a nod. "I have been collaborating with a technology startup, and the experience has been highly unpredictable and exciting."

We have experienced both positive and negative moments, but the overall outcome has been valuable.

They dedicated the following hour to exchanging anecdotes about their professional trajectories, the locations they had travelled to, and the individuals they had encountered during their journeys. Victoria discussed the difficulties and benefits of her occupation, including the long hours dedicated to revising manuscripts and the excitement of witnessing a book she contributed to achieve great success. Joseph detailed his encounters with the startup, the cutting-edge advancements they were pursuing, and the thrill of witnessing the fruits of their labour.

During their conversation, they realised that they shared more similarities than they had originally anticipated. Both individuals had seen growth and transformation during the years, although their fundamental essence remained unaltered. They chuckled over their shared recollections, admired the extent of their individual achievements, and took comfort in the realisation that, despite the passage of time, they still comprehended one other at a fundamental level.

The Initial Ignition

As the talk progressed, Victoria had a growing sense of relaxation. She observed the small details about Joseph that she had previously adored—the inclination of his body when he was genuinely engaged in her conversation, the gleam in his eyes while discussing his passions, and the tender, playful smile that graced his lips when he cracked a joke.

Joseph, also, experienced a strong attraction towards Victoria that he couldn't ignore. He had great admiration for her self-assurance, the manner in which she expressed fervour for her profession, and the radiance that illuminated her eyes when she laughed. He longed for the familiarity of their effortless conversation, their ability to discuss any topic, and the solace of being in the presence of someone who genuinely comprehended him.

"Do you recall the occasion when we became disoriented in the forest while on that educational excursion?" Joseph inquired, amused by the recollection.

Victoria chuckled, while shaking her head. "How did I fail to remember?" We believed that we would remain stranded in that location indefinitely.

"We were extremely obstinate, adamantly refusing to seek assistance," Joseph remarked, beaming. "However, we eventually managed to return."

"Indeed, we did," Victoria responded, her smile becoming gentler. "We consistently discovered a solution, did we not?"

The dialogue had a more intimate tenor as they recollected their mutual history, the escapades they experienced, and the aspirations they previously harboured for the future. They engaged in discussions regarding their families, acquaintances, and pivotal experiences that had influenced their personal development.

An unmistakable chemistry, characterised by a faint yet obvious intensity, permeated the air between them. It was as though the passage of time had vanished, and they were once more the two youthful idealists who had developed romantic feelings for each other during their time in secondary education.

As the day transitioned into nighttime, the café gradually became less crowded. Victoria and Joseph hesitated, both reluctant to conclude the talk at this moment. The sky outside grew dim, and the urban lights commenced to flicker, emitting a cosy radiance through the windows. Joseph reclined in his chair, his attention fixed unwaveringly on Victoria. "I am genuinely pleased that we have undertaken this," he whispered.

"Likewise," Victoria responded, feeling her heart thumping in her chest. "It is satisfying to reestablish a connection."

A brief period of quiet ensued, filled with intense, unexpressed feelings. Both individuals were aware that this was merely the initial stage, and that there remained a great deal to investigate and comprehend about one another. However, at the moment, they were satisfied with proceeding gradually, enjoying the revival of a bond that had never fully been severed.

Upon their departure, Joseph extended his hand and delicately grasped Victoria's. "Shall we arrange to repeat this in the near future?" he inquired, his voice filled with optimism.

Victoria firmly grasped his hand, displaying a joyful expression on her face. "I would appreciate that," she expressed.

They exited the café simultaneously, with the night air enveloping them in a refreshing and chilly manner. Upon their separation, both individuals experienced a revitalised feeling of optimism and anticipation for the possibilities that lie ahead. The rekindling of their connection had revitalised their relationship, and they were eager to explore the possibilities of this renewed opportunity for love.

Chapter Four

Conflicts And Challenges

After a few weeks, Victoria and Joseph had reestablished contact and their developing relationship was starting to form. They dedicated additional time to each other, engaging in activities such as city exploration, communal dining, and rekindling their appreciation for one another. However, once the initial euphoria subsided, the unsolved concerns from their history started to emerge. The interaction commenced with an informal discussion regarding their experiences during their time in secondary education. They were seated in a comfortable nook of Victoria's flat, partaking in a bottle of wine and recollecting memories of past acquaintances.

"Have you ever contemplated the potential consequences if our relationship had not ended?" Victoria inquired, her voice gentle yet inquisitive.

Joseph paused, perceiving the latent unease in her inquiry.

"I acknowledge," he confessed. "However, Victoria, we were rather young at that time. Both of us had aspirations that were leading us in divergent paths. Victoria exhaled audibly, placing her glass on the surface. "I understand, however, it continues to cause pain." Occasionally, I contemplate whether we could have exerted more effort and discovered a solution to successfully maintain our relationship.

Joseph's countenance became taut. "Do you believe that I did not exert sufficient effort?" I made significant sacrifices in order to obtain that scholarship, Victoria. It held significance for my future.

"What are the prospects for our future?" Victoria retorted, her voice escalating. "Did that not concern you?" The dispute rapidly intensified as both individuals reopened past grievances that had never been resolved. The separation unleashed a torrent of unspoken words, brimming with years of suppressed feelings. They engaged in accusations, defences, and infliction of harm upon one another, reenacting the pain from their previous experiences, which overshadowed their current situation. Ultimately, a profound stillness settled in. Both individuals were fatigued and emotionally depleted as a result of the confrontation.

"Apologies," Joseph said softly, his voice shattering the silence. "My intention was not to do you harm. I believed that my actions were in the best interest of both parties involved.

Victoria acknowledged with a nod, her eyes welling up with tears. "I am aware." I desire that circumstances had been altered.

Obstacles from the outside

While traversing the rugged landscape of their revived love, fresh obstacles started to arise. Joseph's occupation necessitated a significant amount of his time, frequently including travel or extended work hours. Victoria's profession was equally challenging, characterised by strict time limits and lofty standards set by her publishing company.

On a specific evening, following an especially demanding week, they had arranged to dine together. Victoria had dedicated the entire to meticulously cooking an exceptional lunch, eagerly anticipating a tranquil evening with Joseph. While she was arranging the table, her phone vibrated with a text message from him. Apologies, Victoria. Was delayed at work. Uncertain about the time of my departure. Can we postpone our plans due to the rain?The text is enclosed in ** tags. Victoria felt a sudden and intense feeling of disappointment or sadness. She comprehended the demands of his occupation, nonetheless, the frequent cancellations and missed arrangements were beginning to have a negative impact. She experienced feelings of neglect, contemplating whether their connection held significance to Joseph or if it was merely one of many items on his extensive list of priorities.

Her exasperation intensified when she encountered Joseph's relatives during a weekend gathering. Despite her politeness, his mother subtly expressed her dislike of Victoria through various comments. She doubted Victoria's dedication to her profession and implicitly implied that Joseph required a partner who could uphold his ambitious way of life.

Victoria experienced a sense of not belonging, with her lack of confidence amplified by the critical looks and indirect comments. She attempted to dismiss it, but the encounter left her feeling more hesitant about their future as a couple.

Uncertainty and Indecision

Victoria and Joseph experienced times of uncertainty and indecision as a result of these issues. They had a deep affection for one another, but they anticipated numerous challenges on their journey ahead. Victoria began to doubt the compatibility of their relationship. The lingering anguish from their previous experiences, combined with the pressures of their current circumstances, caused her to question the appropriateness of reigniting their love affair. Joseph, also, was tormented by uncertainties. He was concerned that his professional aspirations were not consistent with a steady and satisfying romantic partnership. He was reluctant to do harm to Victoria once more, but he was also unwilling to give up the prospects he had diligently pursued. The equilibrium appeared elusive, and he harboured apprehensions that they may be predisposing themselves to yet another emotional setback. While seated on Victoria's balcony, gazing at the city below, the burden of their uncertainties grew too much to disregard. The quiet that existed between them was filled with a palpable sense of unexpressed anxieties. "Joseph," Victoria commenced, her voice quivering. "Do you believe that we are committing an error?" Joseph gazed at her, feeling a profound sense of emotional pain as he observed the lack of conviction reflected in her eyes. "I confess my lack of knowledge," he said. "I desire for this to be successful, but I am experiencing fear." Fearful of the possibility that we will once again cause harm to one another.

Victoria acknowledged with a nod, her eyes filling with tears. "I am also experiencing fear." I am reluctant to part ways with you, yet, I am uncertain if I possess the emotional strength to endure another instance of heartache.

They remained still, grasping each other's hands, both seeking solutions that eluded them. The affection between them was unquestionable, but so were the obstacles they encountered. As they saw the illuminated cityscape, they were aware of the challenging choice they faced: whether to persist in their pursuit of a second opportunity or to relinquish it and proceed with their lives. The future was filled with uncertainty, but it was evident that they could no longer evade the difficult discussions. They were required to confront their concerns, engage in open communication, and collectively determine the course of their destiny. Only after careful evaluation could they ascertain whether their affection possessed the fortitude to surmount the disputes and obstacles impeding their path.

Chapter Five

Recovering Love

While Victoria and Joseph dealt with the intricacies of their revived relationship, they found that despite the difficulties and uncertainties, there were instances of sheer happiness and intimacy. They derived comfort from the uncomplicated joys of being in one other's company and rekindling the mutual hobbies that had initially strengthened their bond.

On a bright Saturday morning, they made the choice to return to the park where they had enjoyed numerous picnics in their high school years. They assembled a hamper containing sandwiches, fruit, and a bottle of effervescent water, and embarked on a day of leisure and nostalgic reflection.

Victoria smiled as Joseph unpacked a frisbee from his luggage while they laid a blanket under the shade of an ancient oak tree. "Do you recall the times when we would spend a considerable amount of time throwing this object back and forth?" he remarked, as he threw it towards her while wearing a smile.

Victoria effortlessly caught it, while laughing. "Certainly!" Your ambition has always been exceptional. They engaged in an afternoon of leisurely activities, including playing frisbee, sharing laughter, and engaging in conversations on various topics. They recollected their most cherished recollections from high school, exchanged anecdotes about their companions and educators, and expressed awe at the considerable transformations that had occurred since that time.

As the sun sank and coloured the sky with shades of pink and orange, Victoria experienced a feeling of tranquilly. Being in the presence of Joseph evoked a sense of ease, comfort, and alignment. Despite growing up and experiencing life separately, their relationship remained intact.

Assistance Systems

Their reunion did not escape the attention of their acquaintances and loved ones. Upon Victoria and Joseph's initial announcement of their reunion, the responses were varied. Many individuals displayed elation and enthusiasm, delighted to see the reunion of two individuals for whom they had deep affection. Some individuals expressed their anxieties, recalling the emotional distress caused by their previous separation and doubting the correctness of their current choice.

Sarah, Victoria's closest companion, was a staunch advocate for her. During a coffee meeting, Sarah attentively listened as Victoria described the successes and challenges of her rekindled romance with Joseph. "I find it marvellous, Em," Sarah expressed, displaying a pleasant smile. "There has always been a unique connection between you and Joseph." Perhaps on this occasion, both of you will be prepared to successfully establish a functional relationship.

Victoria acknowledged, appreciative of Sarah's steadfast backing. "I acknowledge that I have a hopeful expectation," she confessed. "Although it may be challenging, I am hopeful that we can reconcile and reconnect." Michael, Joseph's sibling, responded with a more prudent attitude. During a basketball game in the backyard, Michael conveyed his apprehensions regarding Joseph's demanding work schedule and its potential repercussions on his relationship with Victoria.

"Joseph, be cautious not to disregard her," Michael cautioned, while dribbling the ball. "You have established a successful situation here." Do not allow it to escape once more.

Joseph nodded contemplatively, assimilating his brother's comments. He acknowledged Michael's correctness; achieving a harmonious equilibrium between his professional aspirations and his romantic involvement with Victoria would necessitate diligence and willingness to make concessions. However, he was resolute in his commitment to succeed this time, in order to demonstrate to Victoria that he was really dedicated. Victoria and Joseph found solace and direction in the support of their loved ones as they faced the uncertainty of their revived relationship. They provided counsel, attentively listened, and reiterated the presence of the affection and assistance that enveloped them.

Increasing Fondness

Over time, Victoria and Joseph's friendship grew more profound in ways they hadn't expected. They had a resurgence of love, uncovering previously unknown aspects of each other's characters and reigniting the intense feelings that had previously characterised their relationship.

On a wet evening, Joseph pleasantly surprised Victoria with tickets to a jazz concert—a genre that they had both appreciated but had not yet experienced together. Victoria experienced a feeling of warmth in her chest as she sat next to someone in a dimly lit setting, listening to soothing tunes and drinking wine.

"This is flawless," she whispered, resting her head on Joseph's shoulder.

He gently pressed his lips to the crown of her head, feeling a surge of deep fondness in his heart. "I am pleased that you share that sentiment," he responded in a gentle tone. "I desire for us to experience occasions similar to this, Victoria." Instances of intimate companionship between you and myself.

Victoria beamed, experiencing a surge of appreciation. Unexpectedly, she found herself experiencing a renewed affection for Joseph, as they embarked on a journey of rekindling their love, relishing in the pleasure of companionship, and seeing a shared future. Their affection grew more profound as time went on, bolstered by their collective encounters, their reciprocal admiration, and their steadfast dedication to one another. They acquired the ability to engage in honest and transparent communication, to provide unwavering encouragement for each other's aspirations, and to deeply value the time they spent in each other's company.

While dancing beneath the stars on a balmy summer night, Victoria gazed into Joseph's eyes and realised that their love had never truly diminished. It had become more resilient, enduring the test of time and difficulties, yet unwavering in its loyalty.

They had reunited, rekindling a profound and significant love that surpassed their wildest expectations. Embracing one another amidst the enchanting melodies and captivating atmosphere, they were certain that their love would endure this time.

Chapter Six

Instances Of Intimacy

Victoria felt a strong sense of anticipation as she stood outside the charming Italian restaurant where Joseph had booked reservations for their first official date since they got back together. Anxiously, she straightened her clothes, feeling butterflies fluttering in her tummy. The experience evoked a sense of nostalgia, as the anticipation of a fresh start intertwined with the comfort of familiar emotions, reminiscent of their high school days.

Upon Joseph's arrival, he greeted her with a radiant smile that illuminated his entire countenance. "You appear aesthetically pleasing," he said gently, extending his arm as a gesture of support.

Victoria's face turned red as she experienced a surge of heat in response to his comment. "I appreciate your gesture," she responded, intertwining her arm with his as they entered the restaurant in unison.

The interior exuded a snug and amorous ambiance, as gentle candlelight enveloped the tables in a comforting radiance. They occupied a secluded seat, partaking in a bottle of wine and recollecting their preferred Italian cuisine.

"I recall the initial occasion when we sampled tiramisu," Victoria remarked, chuckling at the recollection. "We were unable to cease discussing the remarkable nature of it." Joseph emitted a light, amused laugh, while his eyes gleamed with excitement. "Subsequently, we dedicated the remaining hours of the evening to endeavouring to replicate the aforementioned experience within the confines of our own residence."

While relishing their lunch, they engaged in a seamless conversation, discussing a wide range of topics. They engaged in a conversation about their aspirations for the future, their preferred literature and films, and the destinations they still desired to explore in one other's company.

Upon the arrival of the dessert, a rich and indulgent slice of tiramisu, they exchanged a meaningful smile. It served as a reminder of their collective past, symbolising the pleasant moments they had treasured together previously and the ones they aspired to build in the future.

Confidential Dialogues

As Victoria and Joseph's friendship grew stronger, they were increasingly inclined towards intimate moments of openness and sincerity. Their chats, which had always been open and unrestricted, suddenly had a more profound meaning as they delved into their aspirations, anxieties, and aspirations for the future.

On a wet Sunday afternoon, they snuggled together on Victoria's couch, covered in blankets, holding hot cups of tea. The gentle sound of raindrops tapping on the windows created a calming atmosphere as they engaged in a conversation about their respective families and the insights gained from previous romantic experiences. "I never anticipated having another opportunity with you," Joseph confessed softly, his eyes locked into Victoria's countenance.

Victoria extended her arm and grasped his hand, applying a gentle pressure. "I also did not," she said. "However, I am extremely pleased that we have managed to reconnect with one another."

They discussed their apprehensions of duplicating previous errors, their hesitations over what lies ahead, and their deepening affection for one another. Victoria expressed her aspirations of establishing a family in the future, of constructing a household brimming with affection and merriment. Joseph listened intently, feeling a surge of affection and inclusion.

During their exclusive discussions, they unearthed a profound connection—a relationship that surpassed mere physical attraction or common interests. They derived peace from embracing each other, found comfort in their mutual vulnerabilities, and gained strength from their steadfast support for one another.

Physical Link

Unanticipatedly, the initial kiss occurred in the evening outside Victoria's flat following a night of watching films. The atmosphere was invigorating with the anticipation of autumn, as the couple strolled together, feeling the satisfying sound of leaves under their feet.

Joseph abruptly halted, pivoting towards Victoria with a tentative grin. "Victoria, there is something I have desired to accomplish since we reestablished contact," he uttered gently.

Prior to Victoria's response, Joseph inclined towards her and bestowed a gentle kiss, his lips exuding warmth and tenderness as they met hers. The kiss was imbued with a profound yearning that had accumulated over the course of many years. It silently conveyed a pledge to reclaim all that they had lost and to go on a journey of rediscovery together.

Victoria's heart accelerated as she reciprocated the kiss, her fingers entwined in his hair. In that instant, the world receded, leaving only the two individuals. This particular moment was a unique blend of excitement and familiarity. After they eventually separated, they stared at one other with a sense of awe, their eyes connecting in a wordless recognition. It marked a pivotal moment in their relationship, a tangible expression of the affection and need that had been growing between them.

During the subsequent days and weeks, their physical bond intensified, with their kisses becoming more fervent and their touches more gentle. They examined each other with a feeling of amazement and admiration, uncovering novel methods to articulate their affection and longing. Their intimacy encompassed both physical and emotional aspects, serving as a manifestation of their growing connection. They embraced one other throughout moments of both joy and sadness, shared intimate secrets during the peacefulness of the night, and experienced the delight of rediscovering love in its most genuine state. While they were intertwined in each other's embrace one night, Victoria experienced a profound feeling of tranquilly. Their path had been replete with fluctuations, uncertainties, and obstacles, but at that particular moment, none of those things held any significance. They successfully reunited, rekindling a love that beyond their expectations in terms of strength and longevity.

As they fell asleep, enfolded in each other's arms, they were aware that their tale of love was only commencing.

Chapter Seven

Overcoming Obstacles

Victoria and Joseph recognised that facing the unresolved issues from their past was essential in order to forward in their revived love. They dedicated numerous late evenings to discussing the factors that led to their initial separation, specifically addressing the unsolved matters that contributed to their breakdown.

On a particular Saturday afternoon, they made the choice to embark on a journey to the town of their upbringing—a location abundant with recollections, both pleasant and unpleasant. They revisited the park where they had previously enjoyed picnics together and the school where they had initially encountered each other, enabling themselves to nostalgically experience experiences from their past.

Perched on a seat with a view of the lake, Victoria initiated the conversation, her voice revealing a hint of vulnerability. "Joseph, I have been contemplating extensively about the events that transpired between us," she said, her gaze unwaveringly focused on the lake. "Upon reflection, I acknowledge that I could have exhibited greater empathy towards your aspirations and goals."

Joseph acknowledged with a solemn expression. "I acknowledge that I could have been more thoughtful towards your feelings," he confessed. "I exerted excessive effort towards my personal objectives without considering the potential consequences for our collective well-being."

They engaged in candid discussions regarding the errors they had committed, the misinterpretations that had caused their separation, and the enduring anguish they had each endured. Revisiting those traumatic memories was challenging, but as they spoke and shed tears, they experienced a sense of relief as a burden lifted from their shoulders.

Through collectively confronting their past, Victoria and Joseph achieved resolution and a revitalised comprehension. They came to the realisation that they were no longer the identical individuals who had separated years ago—that they had developed and become more mature, prepared to construct a future founded on mutual admiration and concession.

Establishing Confidence

Another crucial milestone in their road towards establishing an enduring partnership was the process of restoring trust. Victoria and Joseph actively choose to be open and honest with each other, freely expressing their opinions, concerns, and insecurities without holding back. They developed transparent channels of communication, allocating time for periodic check-ins to discuss their emotions and resolve any emerging difficulties. Victoria valued Joseph's endeavours to involve her in his decision-making process, whether it pertained to professional obligations or personal aspirations. Similarly, Joseph appreciated Victoria's sincerity and dedication to their relationship, recognising that she always provided him with support.

During a calm supper at Joseph's flat one evening, they engaged in an open and honest discussion regarding trust. Victoria uttered her comments in a gentle manner, imbuing them with genuine sincerity. "Joseph, I desire a complete and unwavering trust between us," she stated, her stare resolute. "I desire a sense of security in our relationship, where we can depend on each other unconditionally." Joseph extended his arm across the table and grasped her hand, his eyes mirroring his resolute mindset. "I assure you, Victoria, that I will consistently uphold honesty," he responded sincerely. "I assure you that you can place your trust in me, as I am fully dedicated to ensuring the success of our endeavour."

Their endeavour to restore confidence was not devoid of difficulties. Amidst periods of uncertainty and vulnerability, past traumas returned unexpectedly. However, Victoria and Joseph relied on each other for solace and assistance throughout. They acquired the ability to provide each other personal freedom when necessary, to attentively hear without forming opinions, and to show mercy by pardoning previous errors.

Networks of Support

During their path of surmounting challenges, Victoria and Joseph relied on their supportive networks of friends and family. Their close family and friends played a crucial part in assisting them in managing the intricacies of their revived relationship, providing guidance, support, and emotional comfort at challenging moments. Sarah, Victoria's closest companion, remained a steadfast source of support, providing constant encouragement and cheering them on throughout their journey. She attentively listened to Victoria's concerns and wholeheartedly embraced their achievements with sincere excitement. "You two are destined to be together," Sarah frequently proclaimed, her eyes gleaming with unwavering certainty. Do not allow any obstacles or individuals to interfere with your goals or relationships.

Michael, Joseph's sibling, also played a pivotal role in their expedition. He provided pragmatic guidance and insight, emphasising the need of prioritising his relationship with Victoria amid the demands of his professional life.

"Joseph, do not underestimate her," Michael would caution during their weekly basketball games. "She possesses unique qualities, and it is imperative that you demonstrate your appreciation for her on a daily basis." Victoria and Joseph benefited from the input of their friends and family, who acted as a sounding board, providing diverse viewpoints and assisting them in overcoming their own uncertainties and anxieties. The progress made by Victoria and Joseph was honoured, with support provided during times of doubt and their achievements as a pair being applauded. Victoria and Joseph discovered that their love triumphed over all the hurdles they encountered as they persevered together. As they successfully overcame each obstacle, their bond strengthened, their ability to recover improved, and their dedication to constructing a shared future deepened. They confronted their previous experiences, established trust through transparent communication, and relied on their supportive connections for advice and motivation.

Although their voyage was not yet complete, Victoria and Joseph felt prepared to confront any challenges that lay ahead, as they clasped hands and gazed ahead with determination.

Chapter Eight

Deepening Commitment

After overcoming past obstacles and building a foundation of trust, Victoria and Joseph found themselves contemplating the future of their relationship. They knew it was time to have a serious conversation about where they saw themselves heading together.

One evening, as they strolled hand in hand through a local park illuminated by the soft glow of streetlights, Victoria broached the topic gently. "Joseph, I've been thinking about us," she began, her voice steady but filled with emotion. "Where do you see us going from here?"

Joseph glanced at her, his expression thoughtful. He had been pondering the same question himself, unsure of how to articulate his feelings without sounding too presumptuous. "I want us to be together, Victoria," he replied honestly. "I see a future with you. I want to build a life together."

Victoria smiled, relief washing over her. "I feel the same way, Joseph," she admitted, squeezing his hand. "I want us to be committed to each other, to support each other's dreams and aspirations."

With their hearts laid bare, Victoria and Joseph defined their relationship—a commitment to each other's happiness and well-being, a promise to communicate openly and honestly, and a shared vision for their future.

Planning Together

As their commitment deepened, Victoria and Joseph eagerly began making plans for their future together. They talked about vacations they wanted to take—a romantic getaway to Paris, exploring the beaches of Hawaii, and hiking in the mountains of Colorado.

One lazy Sunday afternoon, they spread out a map on Victoria's coffee table, markers in hand as they discussed their travel bucket list. They laughed as they debated which destination to visit first, envisioning themselves immersed in new cultures, trying new foods, and creating memories that would last a lifetime.

"We have to go to Italy," Joseph insisted, tracing a route along the map. "We can revisit the places we loved and discover new ones together."

Victoria nodded enthusiastically, her eyes sparkling with excitement. "And Greece," she added, pointing to a cluster of islands. "Imagine exploring the ancient ruins and relaxing on the beautiful beaches."

They also talked about more practical matters, like moving in together. Joseph had been looking at apartments closer to Victoria's neighborhood, eager to take the next step in their relationship. They discussed what they wanted in a home—cozy evenings by the fireplace, a kitchen filled with laughter and shared meals, and a space that felt like their sanctuary.

Planning together gave Victoria and Joseph a sense of unity and purpose, solidifying their commitment to building a life filled with love, adventure, and shared dreams.

Symbolic Gestures

As their relationship deepened, Victoria and Joseph began to express their growing commitment to each other through small, meaningful gestures. They exchanged thoughtful gifts—a book Victoria had been wanting to read, a framed photograph of their favorite vacation spot, and handwritten notes filled with words of love and encouragement.

One rainy afternoon, Joseph surprised Victoria with a bouquet of her favorite flowers—a simple gesture that brightened her day and reminded her of his thoughtfulness and affection.

Victoria, in turn, surprised Joseph with tickets to a baseball game—a sport they both loved but had never attended together. They cheered for their favorite team, sharing popcorn and laughter as they bonded over their mutual love for the game.

They also started wearing matching bracelets—a symbol of their commitment to each other, a reminder of the love and respect they shared.

These symbolic gestures reinforced Victoria and Joseph's deepening connection, reaffirming their commitment to each other in tangible ways. They celebrated their milestones, cherished their shared experiences, and looked forward to a future filled with love, joy, and endless possibilities.

As they stood hand in hand, gazing at the stars one clear summer night, Victoria and Joseph knew that their journey together was just beginning. They had defined their relationship, made plans for their future, and expressed their commitment through meaningful gestures. And as they embraced under the twinkling sky, they knew that their love story was one of resilience, hope, and the beauty of second chances fulfilled.

Chapter Nine

The major Conflict

Victoria and Joseph, despite their growing dedication and common aspirations, had a significant conflict that challenged the resilience of their partnership. The conflict arose from a divergence of views over a consequential choice that had implications for their respective futures. During a supper at Joseph's flat one evening, they discussed the topic that had been preoccupying their thoughts for weeks: whether or not to cohabitate. Joseph discovered an ideal flat in close proximity to Victoria's neighbourhood, perceiving it as a significant progression in their relationship.

Victoria paused, her mind in a state of confusion as she pondered the consequences. "Joseph, I have deep affection for you and I desire for us to form a romantic partnership," she continued cautiously. "However, I am uncertain about whether it is currently the optimal choice for me to cohabitate."

Joseph's face contorted with displeasure, taken aback by her unexpected reply. "However, Victoria, we have previously discussed this matter." "We both desire to progress further," he asserted in a gentle manner. "What is causing your hesitation?"

Victoria let out a deep breath, experiencing conflicting emotions. "I genuinely desire to be with you," she explained sincerely. "I simply require additional time to adapt." "I am not yet prepared to relinquish my autonomy entirely."

Their discussion became intense as they deliberated the advantages and disadvantages of cohabitation. Victoria articulated her desire for personal autonomy and freedom, while Joseph experienced emotional pain and bewilderment due to his interpretation of her apparent hesitancy to totally devote herself to their relationship. The dispute intensified, their voices crescendoing with fervour as they grappled to discover mutual agreement. Victoria left Joseph's flat after a heated exchange of hurtful words, seeking solitude to reflect on her emotions.

Interim Disconnection

After their intense dispute, Victoria and Joseph experienced a period of temporary separation. During this time, they engaged in self-reflection and faced uncertainty, which challenged their determination and loyalty to each other.

Victoria found comfort in extended strolls along the riverbank, as the refreshing wind brought her a feeling of mental clarity amidst the emotional upheaval she was experiencing. She grappled with contradictory sentiments—affection for Joseph, apprehension of losing her identity inside the relationship, and ambiguity regarding their prospective union. Meanwhile, Joseph engrossed himself in his job, attempting to divert his attention from the pain caused by their quarrel. He longed for Victoria intensely, his heart burdened with remorse for their passionate arguments and the growing rift between them.

Their acquaintances and relatives provided assistance and counsel, encouraging them to engage in transparent and sincere communication on their emotions. However, Victoria and Joseph required a period of time to mentally and emotionally analyse their feelings and discover a path towards reconciliation on their own conditions.

Epiphany

Over the course of several weeks, Victoria and Joseph each engaged in a process of self-reflection, delving deeply into their own emotions and thoughts. This introspective journey ultimately resulted in a profound understanding of their deep affection for one another. One night, illuminated by the gentle radiance of a street lamp, Victoria found herself positioned outside Joseph's flat, her heart throbbing with indecisiveness. Taking a profound inhalation, she mustered the bravery to rap on his door.

Joseph responded, displaying a fleeting expression of astonishment and relief at seeing her. "Victoria," he said, his voice raspy with sentiment. "I have longed for your presence."

Victoria acknowledged with a nod, her eyes welling up with tears. "I also missed you, Joseph," she said in a gentle manner. "After much contemplation, I have come to the realisation that I was experiencing fear." I am apprehensive about losing my sense of myself inside our connection, and I am hesitant to progress farther without absolute certainty.

Joseph attentively listened, feeling a deep sense of empathy and sorrow. "I apologise for exerting force on you," he expressed really. "Victoria, I have strong affection for you." I desire for us to be in a relationship, but only if it aligns with your genuine desires as well. Victoria nodded, experiencing a profound feeling of lucidity. "Indeed," she responded sincerely. "Joseph, I also have strong affection for you." "I desire for us to collaboratively solve this issue at our preferred speed." During that instance of vulnerability and sincerity, Victoria and Joseph came to the realisation that their love was worth defending—that despite their disparities and anxieties, they were more resilient when united rather than separated. They confronted their most significant disagreement directly, endured the period of temporary separation, and emerged with a heightened comprehension of themselves and one another. As they hugged, their hearts intertwined once again, Victoria and Joseph were aware that their love story was still ongoing. They had acquired vital insights regarding communication, negotiation, and the significance of respecting one another's wants and desires. Their journey was characterised by adversities and personal development, however they found that their love was robust, lasting, and able to conquer even the most formidable hurdles. As they gazed ahead, holding hands, they understood that their love story was only starting—a demonstration of the potency of forgiveness, self-reflection, and the profound impact of genuine love.

Chapter Ten

Reconciliation

Following their resolution of a significant fight and brief period of being apart, Victoria and Joseph encountered a critical juncture—a decisive moment that would shape the trajectory of their relationship. They had encountered their anxieties, challenged their insecurities, and emerged with increased strength and dedication.

Victoria and Joseph rendezvoused at their cherished café, a location imbued with recollections of mirth and mutual aspirations, on a cool autumn afternoon. They were seated facing one other, with their hands entwined, their eyes mirroring a blend of affection, resolve, and optimism.

"I apologise, Joseph," Victoria said gently, her voice brimming with genuine sincerity. "I have come to the realisation that I allowed my fears to hinder our progress."

I have strong affection for you and I desire for our relationship to continue.

Joseph extended his arm across the table and tenderly applied pressure to her hand, feeling a surge of comfort and affection in his heart. "Victoria, I reciprocate your love," he responded sincerely. "I apologise for exerting force on you." I desire for us to go at a suitable tempo, constructing a shared future that both of us find agreeable. During the time of reconciliation, Victoria and Joseph openly acknowledged their vulnerabilities and joyfully commemorated their reinvigorated dedication to one another. They had acquired the knowledge of the significance of patience, comprehension, and unwavering affection—a basis on which they would construct their enduringly blissful future.

Significant Display

In order to symbolise their reconciliation and solidify their dedication to one another, Joseph devised an elaborate display of affection—a heartfelt demonstration that would encapsulate the profound extent of his love and loyalty for Victoria.

Joseph pleasantly surprised Victoria by arranging a romantic meal illuminated by candles on the rooftop patio of an exclusive hotel, providing a picturesque view of the city skyline. Amidst the ambiance of soft melodies, they indulged in a refined culinary experience, engaging in lively discourse and fond recollections.

Under the shimmering night sky, Joseph rose and approached Victoria, gently grasping her hands. "Victoria," he continued, his voice unwavering yet brimming with sentiment. "Upon our reunion, I immediately recognised that you were the individual with whom I desired to share the entirety of my existence."

He knelt down, holding a little velvet box, and gazed into Victoria's eyes with absolute conviction. "Victoria, would you consent to becoming my spouse?" Would you bestow upon me the privilege of becoming your life partner? Victoria's eyes filled with tears as she looked at Joseph, her heart brimming with love and happiness. "Indeed, Joseph," she said, her voice quivering with intense affection. "Certainly, I wholeheartedly agree."

Their hug was brimming with emotions of elation and mirth, as they commemorated their affection and the prospect of a shared destiny. Joseph placed the ring on Victoria's finger, symbolising their dedication, affection, and pursuit of a blissful future together.

Future Commitments

In the concluding epilogue of their romantic tale, Victoria and Joseph eagerly anticipated their future with enthusiasm and expectation. They organised their wedding—an event commemorating their affection, with the presence of relatives and friends who had provided them with assistance during their experience. They discussed their aspirations for the future, which included a comfortable residence brimming with affection and joy, trips to both unfamiliar and familiar destinations, and eventually establishing their own family. Victoria enthusiastically pursued her passion for photography, skillfully capturing moments of happiness and affection that enriched their lives. Joseph consistently thrived in his profession, bolstered by Victoria's steadfast support and affection.

Their loved ones celebrated their joy, commemorating the love story that triumphed over challenges and blossomed into a beautiful and lasting bond. Victoria and Joseph were aware that their ongoing path would be marked by both difficulties and successes, but they had faith in their affection and dedication to one another. Underneath a starry canopy on a balmy summer evening, Victoria and Joseph, holding hands, realised that they had discovered their enduring happiness—a tale of love crafted with patience, determination, and unshakeable trust in one another. With their gaze fixed on the future, brimming with hope and thankfulness, they were certain that their love would perpetually flourish, intensify, and brighten their lives.

Chapter Eleven

Accepting Vulnerability

Victoria and Joseph engage in profound conversations that beyond the commonplace, while sitting in the tranquil and comfortable ambiance of Victoria's cosy living room, surrounded by the gentle radiance of candles. With cautious yet resolute tones, they commence to divulge the profound depths of their emotions, revealing concealed secrets and vulnerabilities that have been harboured for a long time.

Victoria inhales deeply, her hands quivering slightly as she recounts a childhood characterised by bereavement and a dread of being deserted. Joseph patiently listens, his eyes mirroring empathy and comprehension as he recognises the profound impact of these early experiences on Victoria's worries and insecurities. Joseph reciprocates by discussing his personal challenges with self-doubt and the burden of meeting the demands imposed on him. He discloses instances of vulnerability that he has hardly discussed, acknowledging the burden of responsibility he has silently borne for years. During their exchange of private revelations, a significant transformation takes place between them. The walls that formerly protected their emotions are now collapsing, giving way to a newfound feeling of closeness and reliance. They derive comfort from each other's vulnerabilities, acknowledging that their shared willingness to be open is not an indication of weakness but of resilience—a demonstration of their strengthening connection and mutual longing for greater comprehension.

Addressing Previous Traumatic Experiences

Victoria and Joseph bravely confront the lingering effects of their prior traumas, which have been exposed and made vulnerable. They confront distressing recollections and psychological injuries that have persisted beneath the surface, impacting their current lives and relationships. Victoria reflects on a significant event from her teenage years, a betrayal that destroyed her confidence and left lasting emotional wounds that have partially healed but nevertheless remain visible. Joseph attentively listens, providing calm reassurance and a reassuring presence as Victoria relates the circumstances with a blend of sadness and relief.

Joseph also has his own inner struggles, which include the lingering effects of a chaotic familial environment that influenced his views on love and dedication. He recognises the influence of these experiences on his capacity to trust and display vulnerability in relationships, imparting insights that enhance Victoria's comprehension of his emotional landscape.

Collectively, they traverse the emotional landscape of their previous traumas with understanding and sympathy, granting one another the opportunity and assistance to mend prior injuries. Amidst emotional tears and intimate moments of solace, they realise that confronting their shared history fortifies their connection and opens the path towards a future imbued with revitalised optimism and fortitude.

Enhancing Their Connection

Victoria and Joseph experience a stronger connection as they willingly expose their vulnerabilities, surpassing their expectations. They have overcome their reluctance of revealing their authentic identities to one another, experiencing liberation and approval within the secure confines of their affection.

Their dialogues evolve into a state of ease, enriched with a newly discovered closeness and reliance that surpasses just verbal communication. They develop a reliance on one another at times of doubt, providing unwavering assistance and motivation as they handle the difficulties of life collectively.

Guided by vulnerability, Victoria and Joseph start on a path of reciprocal personal development and comprehension. They commemorate one another's strengths and vulnerabilities, acknowledging that genuine closeness is established not in flawlessness but in the readiness to be observed and embraced as their own selves. Afterward, Victoria and Joseph take comfort in the understanding that their love is firmly rooted in genuineness and mutual encounters. Their exploration of vulnerability has not only fortified their connection but has also established the groundwork for a future abundant in trust, empathy, and steadfast dedication.

Chapter Twelve

Rediscovering Passion

Victoria and Joseph set out on a quest to rekindle the intensity of their physical bond, acknowledging it as a crucial element of their developing relationship. They engage in intimate experiences that go beyond the purely physical realm, driven by a greater openness and a desire for exploration.

During the tranquil minutes before sunrise, Victoria and Joseph are entwined in each other's embrace, their bodies communicating a profound need and passion that cannot be expressed through words. They experience anew the excitement of physical contact—the gentle contact of fingertips against skin, the comforting warmth of shared breath, and the affectionate glance that communicates unexpressed truths.

Placing a high importance on closeness and emotional connection becomes a fundamental aspect of their everyday routines, whether it be through brief, secretive kisses in the kitchen or lingering, heartfelt hugs before going their separate ways for the day. They deliberately create opportunities to cultivate their physical intimacy, recognising that it not only enhances their desire but also fortifies the emotional connection they have.

Acts of Romance

Joseph pleasantly surprises Victoria with a sequence of impromptu and sincere actions that reignite the passion in their relationship. He astounds her with spontaneous picnics in the park, featuring her preferred delicacies and a blanket arranged beneath the shelter of their beloved oak tree. Every gesture serves as evidence of his keen awareness and the profoundness of his affection. Victoria responds to Joseph's gestures by writing him heartfelt love letters that beautifully encapsulate the spirit of their shared experiences. She reflects on their initial encounter, their early hesitations, and the instances that strengthened their connection. Her heartfelt and candid statements serve as a concrete symbol of their mutual past and the collective future they are constructing.

Collectively, they organise a retreat to a charming coastal village—the exact location where they initially disclosed their emotions several years prior. Strolling together by the shoreline, they reminisce about treasured moments and forge fresh ones, appreciating the splendour of the current instant and the potential of their forthcoming days.

Fostering Mutual Support for Pursuing Personal Aspirations

Victoria and Joseph form a connection based on mutual respect and admiration, supporting and encouraging each other as they work towards their goals and ambitions. Victoria motivates Joseph to pursue his passion project—an exhibition of his photography that highlights his distinct perspective and imaginative vision.

Joseph serves as a reliable source of support for Victoria, assisting her in overcoming instances of self-doubt over her career goals. With steadfast confidence in her capabilities, he intently listens as she divulges her aspirations and provides practical guidance and support.

They commemorate one another's accomplishments, whether significant or minor, with genuine joy and admiration. By engaging in activities like as toasting Joseph's successful exhibition opening and dancing in the living room to honour Victoria's promotion, they cultivate a culture of celebration and support that fosters their personal development and enhances their connection as a couple.

Victoria and Joseph understand that true intimacy is not just about physical proximity, but also about the profound emotional bond and unshakable support they offer each other as they rediscover their passion together. By engaging in romantic gestures and providing reciprocal support, they establish a trajectory characterised by shared hopes, aspirations, and an ever-strengthening love.

Chapter Thirteen

Managing Divergences

Victoria and Joseph face a critical decision point as they imagine their future as a couple, with both of them clinging to aspirations that appear to lead them in separate paths. Victoria aspires to establish a life enriched by familial bonds and nostalgic recollections, firmly anchored in the comfort and familiarity of her birthplace. Meanwhile, Joseph's ambitions propel him towards the vibrant atmosphere and professional prospects of a metropolis. Victoria and Joseph engage in sincere and open discussions, where they express their long-term objectives and ambitions. They skillfully manage the intricacies of compromise, carefully considering many possibilities that uphold their individual aspirations while simultaneously charting a collective course as a unified pair. By engaging in active listening and demonstrating mutual respect, they are able to reach a compromise—a point where Victoria's feeling of belonging aligns with Joseph's desire for personal development, resulting in a shared vision for their future that incorporates the advantages of both perspectives.

Variations in Culture and Individuality

Victoria and Joseph originate from separate cultural heritages, each contributing a diverse array of customs, convictions, and principles to their relationship. By embracing and celebrating their cultural diversity, individuals uncover the beauty of gaining knowledge from one other's distinct viewpoints.

They participate in sincere discussions about how their backgrounds impact their perspective on the world, moulding their convictions towards love, family, and personal identity. Victoria recounts anecdotes about her family's long-standing customs, which have been handed down from one generation to the next, while Joseph candidly discusses the traditions that have influenced his perception of community and cultural heritage. Through these chats, Victoria and Joseph enhance their understanding of the profound cultural diversity inside their relationship. They derive pleasure from amalgamating customs, forging novel ceremonies that pay homage to their own pasts and commemorate the future they are constructing collectively.

Effective Conflict Management

During their travels, Victoria and Joseph face arguments and problems that test their unity. They acknowledge these instances as chances for personal development and comprehension, dedicating themselves to settling disagreements with kindness and understanding. They build tactics for effectively handling disagreement, acquiring the ability to openly and candidly communicate without apprehension of criticism or misinterpretation. Victoria engages in active listening, attentively focusing on Joseph's opinions with sincere interest and a genuine intention to empathise with his viewpoint. Joseph, on the other hand, acquires the ability to articulate his emotions clearly and calmly, guaranteeing that his motives are communicated with affection and admiration. Collectively, they foster an environment of open communication and negotiation, utilising disagreements as a catalyst for establishing stronger bonds and shared comprehension. Victoria and Joseph successfully manage their differences by demonstrating patience, perseverance, and a mutual dedication to their relationship. This not only strengthens their connection but also serves to reinforce their love as they conquer each obstacle they encounter.

Chapter Fourteen

Commemorating Achievements

Victoria and Joseph commemorate their anniversary, reflecting on the profound evolution of their love since their reunion. Seated opposite each other at their preferred bistro, they raise their glasses in celebration of the significant occasions that have shaped their relationship—an embodiment of their ability to endure, maintain optimism, and remain steadfastly dedicated.

They reenact their initial encounter, characterised by anxious amusement and uncertain chemistry, now superseded by a profound and enduring affection that has only intensified over the years. Strolling together in the park where they had their first kiss, they reflect on the significant achievements they have accomplished as a couple—the triumphs and challenges that have influenced their connection.

During a romantic supper with a candle, Victoria and Joseph express appreciation for the experiences they have had together, recognising the difficulties they have encountered and the happiness they have found in each other's embrace. They make sincere vows for the future, confirming their dedication to fostering a love that grows and prospers.

Introducing Our Closest Friends to Each Other

Victoria enthusiastically acquaints Joseph with her closest companions, extending an invitation for him to join the exclusive group that has provided unwavering support over the ups and downs of her life. Amidst the sound of laughter resonating in Victoria's comfortable living room, Joseph becomes enveloped in tales of Victoria's younger years—her mischievous behaviour, her aspirations, and the steadfast devotion of her companions.

Joseph reciprocates by acquainting Victoria with his close-knit circle of acquaintances, recounting stories of companionship and collective experiences that have influenced his personal path. Victoria attentively listens, deriving solace from the companionship and mutual connections that characterise Joseph's social group—a monument to the friendships that have influenced his development into the guy she adores.

During these sessions, Victoria and Joseph enhance their support networks, intertwining the elements of their separate lives into a fabric of common experiences and lasting friendships. They rejoice in the process of merging, aware that their affection is strengthened by the unwavering backing of those who have observed their development and advocated for their well-being.

Contemplating Individual Development

Victoria and Joseph, in solitude, begin on a journey of self-reflection, contemplating the individual development they have undergone since reuniting. Victoria is amazed by the strength she has found within herself - the bravery to accept vulnerability, tackle concerns, and move forward despite not knowing what lies ahead.

Joseph appreciates the insights gained from previous relationships, acknowledging how they have influenced his ability to love and make commitments. He imparts to Victoria the recently acquired lucidity he has obtained - the significance of communication, compromise, and steadfast support in constructing an enduring alliance.

Victoria and Joseph together establish fresh personal and interpersonal objectives for the future, visualising a life abundant with mutual desires and aspirations. They dedicate themselves to cultivating their personal interests while nurturing a love that constantly develops—a demonstration of the progress they have made and the limitless possibilities of their shared future.

Victoria and Joseph express their conviction in the profound impact of love by commemorating significant events such as anniversaries, friendships, and personal development. United in their emotions and thoughts, they eagerly welcome the prospect of a forthcoming existence brimming with happiness, satisfaction, and an infinite love.

Chapter Fifteen

A New Beginning

 Moving Forward

Chapter 15: Constructing an Enduring Heritage

Future Planning

Victoria and Joseph engage in sincere discussions about their mutual future, exploring the thrilling opportunities that await them. They engage in a conversation about marriage, delving into the significance of the institution for each of them. They go beyond the surface level of vows and ceremonies, viewing marriage as a representation of commitment, partnership, and lasting love. United by their deep affection, they imagine a forthcoming time when their connection is strengthened via a sacred union that commemorates their shared experiences.

They engage in conversations around the prospect of beginning a family, reflecting on the pleasures and obligations of being parents. Victoria expresses her aspirations of establishing a warm and affectionate household characterised by joy and the sound of children's footsteps, while Joseph embraces the opportunity to foster and mentor future generations with calmness and sagacity. Collectively, they create an optimal chronological sequence that harmonises their career ambitions with their wish to form a family founded on affection and stability.

The process of establishing a collective vision for their future residence and way of life involves a joint effort, combining Victoria's inclination towards warm and welcoming environments with Joseph's admiration for contemporary amenities and practicality. They create blueprints for a residence that mirrors their individualities—a haven where treasured recollections are formed, customs are respected, and affection flourishes in every nook.

Contributing to the Community

Victoria and Joseph are motivated by a mutual dedication to creating a beneficial influence. They derive satisfaction from volunteering together for causes that are personally meaningful to them. They actively engage in community initiatives, such as volunteering at a local shelter, coordinating fundraising events for educational programmes, and participating in tree planting projects to enhance green areas.

They experience the pleasure of contributing, deriving meaning from acts of benevolence and empathy that elevate others and reinforce the cohesion of their society. Victoria's compassion and understanding perfectly compliment Joseph's unwavering resolve and ingenuity, resulting in a powerful alliance that motivates others to unite in their endeavours to build a more promising future for everyone.

Collectively, they discover inventive methods to make a positive impact on their society, utilising their abilities and interests to bring about significant transformation. They establish collaborations with local organisations, mobilising assistance and cultivating a feeling of solidarity among community members and acquaintances. Victoria and Joseph demonstrate the transforming influence of collective action and the significant effect of philanthropy.

Embracing the Unfamiliar

Victoria and Joseph approach their future with optimism and resilience, despite the uncertainty that lay ahead. They recognise that life is replete with unforeseen changes and challenges, wholeheartedly embracing the path that lies ahead with steadfast belief in their love and dedication to one another.

They anticipate unforeseen obstacles and modifications, acknowledging that their resilience is rooted in their capacity to adjust and develop collectively. Victoria and Joseph view uncertainty as a chance for personal development and education, skillfully handling each challenge with elegance and bravery. They rely on one another for assistance, deriving solace from the understanding that they are joined in their endeavour to achieve a collective future brimming with limitless opportunities.

Victoria and Joseph, filled with curiosity and anticipation, begin the next phase of their life together, prepared to confront any challenges with determination, positivity, and an unshakeable faith in the strength of their affection. Collectively, they construct an enduring heritage—an affirmation of their dedication to one another, their society, and the ongoing expedition they undertake with limitless optimism and resolute bravery.

About the book

Our Second Chance Romance is an endearing story of love reignited despite challenging circumstances. Upon an unexpected reunion, Victoria and Joseph are abruptly immersed in a realm of past recollections and lingering emotions. Their fortuitous encounter establishes the framework for a voyage into their previous experiences, as they wrestle with the sentiments and aspirations they once mutually possessed. Upon each meeting, they are reminded of the profound connection that previously connected them, prompting them to contemplate the possibility of a renewed opportunity for the love they believed was permanently lost.

Victoria and Joseph encounter various obstacles and disputes as they traverse the intricacies of reconnecting, which put their rebuilt relationship to the test. Their journey is filled with challenges, ranging from reigniting physical intimacy and embracing their cultural disparities, to navigating external barriers and overcoming internal fears. However, despite facing various challenges, they draw resilience from their mutual past and develop a stronger bond that surpasses the hardships they face. Their narrative serves as evidence of the enduring strength of affection and the influence of emotional openness, as they acquire the ability to openly express themselves, find common ground, and actively encourage one other's aspirations.

9 798890 361639